AT THE
HOT GATES

AT THE HOT GATES

AN ACCOUNT OF THE
BATTLE OF THERMOPYLAE

BY DONALD SAMSON

WITH ILLUSTRATIONS BY ADAM AGEE

ACKNOWLEDGEMENTS

My thanks to friend and former mentor, Apostolos Athanassakis,
professor of Classics, University of California at Santa Barbara,
who kindly read the manuscript with an eye for historical accuracy.
Any errors or inconsistencies are solely mine.
Also my enduring gratitude to David Mitchell (1945–2012),
editor of AWSNA Publications, whose vision, dedication, depth of
knowledge and generous heart shall be sorely missed
by all those who knew him.

—»» ««—

Printed with support from the Waldorf Curriculum Fund

Published by:
The Association of Waldorf Schools
of North America
Publications Office
38 Main Street
Chatham, NY 12037

Title: *At the Hot Gates*
    An Account of the Battle of Thermopylae
Author: Donald Samson
Designer & Illustrator: Adam Agee
Copy editor & Proofreader: Ann Erwin
Cover: Adam Agee
Text © 2012 by Donald Samson
Illustrations © 2012 by Adam Agee
ISBN #978-1-936367-28-3

Printed by McNaughton & Gunn
Saline, MI 48176 USA

THE BUSHES to my left shook violently and I whirled around to meet the intruder. I clutched my spear in both hands and readied it at eye-level. I steeled myself to drive the point right into his teeth. My full attention was in front of me, so I was taken by surprise when a pair of massive arms suddenly enfolded me from behind in a bear hug. With my arms pinned to my sides, I could only kick with my legs, but it did little good. I was lifted off the ground. I bent my neck to try to bite his arms, but I couldn't reach.

Without loosening his vise grip, he shoved my head hard to the left, and the muscles in my neck screamed in protest. Then I felt the cold metal of the man's helmet pressed against my cheek.

"Get quiet, or I'll break your neck," he growled into my ear.

It was a Spartan voice, so I knew he meant it. I stopped kicking and struggling.

"Now drop the spear," he commanded.

With my arms pinned, my makeshift spear was dangling from my fingertips. I let it drop.

"Real easy now," he said. I thought he was going to let me go. I was ready, the moment my feet touched the ground, to dash through the thicket and escape. Perhaps he sensed my muscles tensing. Whatever the reason, he smashed me to the ground on my face. I was stunned from the blow. Then I felt his knee in my back, pressing the air out of my lungs.

"Stay put!" he ordered.

He roughly grabbed my arms and pulled them behind me. I wondered for a brief moment if he were about to drive his sword between my shoulder blades.

"*Thanatos!*" I prayed silently. "O, Death, come thou quickly that I make no noise to shame me." But instead of thrusting his sword into my back, he dragged me to my feet by my long hair and held on firmly. I struggled again and only now noticed that when he had thrown me to the ground, he had bound my hands behind me.

"What have we here?" spoke a voice. I looked to my left. A large man had stepped out of the bushes, his red cloak hanging loosely from his shoulders. He wore no helmet, but his sword was in his hand. He looked amused and curious. He must have been the one who had shaken the bushes to distract me. That had given the other one a chance to grab me from behind. I decided I could be thankful he had not skewered me on the spot and left me to be feasted upon by scavenging dogs.

"Maybe a spy, Kroton," said the one who had captured me. He still had me by the hair, and I could not turn to see him.

"Don't know, Hamides. He's too naked to be a Persian. Looks Greek to me," Kroton said, holding my chin in his hand and peering into my face.

The man holding me grunted dismissively. "And that means?"

"Not much," the other admitted.

"I'm guessing an escaped slave," the one behind me said. "His back has seen the lash."

"That could mean a slave *and* a spy. And if he's a Greek, there's no trusting him anyway. Let's find out how far away his master is."

Behind me, Hamides took his handful of hair and twisted it, lifting my heels off the ground. I wasn't ready for the pain and a gasp escaped my lips.

"Who's your master, slave?" he snarled into my ear.

"No master," I snarled back through clenched teeth. I was offended at the implication I was a slave. I was completely unprepared for their reaction. Hamides released my hair and gave me a hard shove. With my hands bound behind me, I lost my footing and fell to the ground. Looking up at them, ready to face a sword at my throat, I saw that they were both laughing.

"What's a Spartan pup doing out here?" Hamides asked. They must have seen the amazement on my face.

"Boy, obviously this is your first time away from Sparta," Kroton said. "You have not yet discovered that, although we are surrounded by Greeks who make up both our friends and enemies, we have our own way of speaking. Your accent gives you away."

"So what are you?" Hamides demanded. "A helot slave or a Spartan? Answer me true."

"A Spartan I am."

"Then why have you run away from your *agela*, your youth group? Was it too harsh for you?"

"Didn't run away," I stammered.

Kroton stood a moment in reflection.

"Didn't run away, huh? That means you were running towards. Am I right?"

I had already said too much. I pressed my lips together and remained silent.

"What'll we do with him?" Hamides asked.

"What else? To Leonidas."

Hooking my arms, they trotted me along between them through the thickets.

"How long?" one of them asked. We Spartans are not much on conversation. We speak in few words and often have to guess what the other wants to know. I knew he was asking how long I had been trailing them.

"Since Sparta," I said.

"Good tracking," he said. I took this as a great compliment. I also wanted to know: When had they sensed my presence?

"How long?" I asked in return.

"Five days," he said.

"No!" I shouted. It wasn't possible! They had been on the road for six days. We pride ourselves in being patient hunters, but had they tolerated me following them that long? Then I noticed they were laughing again.

"This morning," Kroton said. "Like I said, good tracking."

"But, once we sniffed you out, you could not elude us for long," Hamides said.

"After all," Kroton added. "We, too, were raised as Spartan boys. We know all the tricks."

They trotted me along, roughly, yet not unkindly. We came into the clearing where the camp was settled. I could smell the food on the cook fires. The strong aroma set my stomach off and it began to growl loudly. I was shamed by it, but had no way to stop it.

"Hungry, boy?"

A Spartan admits no weakness. I remained silent.

"You'll have to steal what you eat."

"And if you're caught, you'll be beaten."

So what was different? I'd been stealing food since I turned seven and was taken away from my mother and my sisters to live with the other boys. My brothers had all gone before me, so I was proud when my turn came. We all stole food in my *agela*. They never fed us enough. They expected us to steal and to learn how to do it without getting caught. The punishment was a flogging—for getting caught, not for stealing. Stealing was how I had stayed alive following the troops. I'd been trained well. I didn't need to eat, anyway.

I looked up at my captors. They were smiling in their beards, as if reading my thoughts. We entered the camp.

"Look what we caught for breakfast," Hamides called out. Eyes glanced up. Many stood and walked over to us. I knew what they wanted to know. I looked around, and, although he was the reason I had come, I dreaded seeing him. For the moment, though, I was saved this disgrace.

"Shall we roast him whole?" one asked.

"I say cut him into little pieces and boil him in a stew. He'll feed more," another said, picking up a knife and testing its edge. "I'm tired of barley cakes. Let's make a black broth out of him."

Their expressions were somber and I could not hear joking in their words. I broke into a cold sweat. One of the men came over to me, peered into my face, and pinched the skin over my ribs between his hard fingers. When I didn't react, he pinched harder. I stared defiantly back into his face, pressing my lips together, but I never flinched. He could rip the skin off, I wasn't going to make a sound.

He snorted and let go. "Spartan flesh makes a lean meal," he commented.

"Give me a fat Persian!" Now there was lots of laughter, and the somber mood I had felt was lifted.

They walked me over to a man sitting on a low boulder. He looked lost in thought, his eyes downcast. His red cape hung about his shoulders. I knew him. Sparta is large, but not so large that we didn't know our kings. Here was Leonidas. He was a legend to us boys. A king of few words among a people of few words. Quick tempered, quick to act, decisive and sure. Men would walk through fire for him. And then they would turn around and walk through a second time if it was needed, because Leonidas would be the first to go. He was trusted, respected, feared and loved. A strange combination perhaps, but among us Spartans, it is our peculiar way.

Leonidas was the king we relied on to take men into the field of battle. Our second king, Leotychides—for Sparta always has two kings, one to go to battle, the other to hold the city—was an older and more deliberate man. He knew how to both manage and manipulate the *Gerousia*, the council of elders. He never acted hastily, and the younger men were annoyed by his slowness. King Leonidas, on the other hand, irritated the elders with his headstrong actions. Like leading his personal fighting contingent to the distant Hot Gates to hold off the greatest army ever to take the field since Agamemnon led the Greeks against Troy.

"We've caught him," Kroton announced. Leonidas looked up, his dark features brightening.

"I suspected as much. That it was just a boy," he said.

"And a Spartan cub at that," Hamides added.

Leonidas gazed at me severely.

"Not an escaped helot?" He sounded surprised. Then he addressed me with a hard look. "Why did you leave your group? Boy, you owe obedience and loyalty to your *agela*. You depend on one another. Why did you run away?"

I didn't answer. I wanted to, but the words wouldn't come.

"Untie his hands," he commanded when I said nothing. I felt Kroton cut through my bonds with his sword.

I reacted to the movement even before I realized that the king had swung his open hand at my head. I dodged and he missed me with that arm, but I wasn't ready for the hard hand coming from the other direction. He knocked me to the ground.

"Get up," he commanded. As I was getting to my feet, he came after me. Even if he is our king, no Spartan will let himself get beaten unless he is ordered to stand still or his hands are tied. And he had ordered mine cut loose.

I dodged out of his way. He lunged at me, and the only way I could turn him aside was a blow with the side of my arm against his head. His head was hard and he was a big man, but it was enough to escape his reach. I leapt to the side.

The king charged at me again and knocked me on my back. He followed up with his whole body. I knew what was coming. If I stayed where I was, he would land with his weight behind his knee right on my chest and squeeze all the life out of me. I twisted out from under him and scrambled to my feet. I went into a crouch and stared at his chest. I could track his next move by watching him there. If he wanted to kill me, I would give him a fight first. I wasn't going to run and I wasn't going to let him pin me down and beat me.

Leonidas, though didn't continue his attack. He stood there with his hands on his hips, a serious look on his face.

"Will you fight your king?" he demanded.

"I will defend myself, o king," I said.

"Will you not bow down before me?" he asked. "Onto your knees," he commanded.

This puzzled me. When did anyone ever bow down to the kings? We followed their orders, we honored them, we trusted them to lead us into battle, but we didn't bow down to them. Ever. Uncertain what he wanted, I shook my head.

"I am a Spartan," I said, trying to make sense of his order.

Leonidas' frown now turned into a broad smile. "That you are, my boy. You've proven that to me beyond doubt."

It began to dawn on me that Leonidas had been testing me.

"Who is your father, boy?"

I said nothing. No one must know.

Leonidas waited, peering at me. Then he nodded his head.

"I see. Well, then tell me why are you here, boy, instead of in your training?"

"I came to fight the Persians," I said.

Here he began to laugh.

"No armor, training unfinished, run away from your *agela*, your loyalty group, but ready to fight. You are a Spartan, and also a fool. But who knows? Perhaps the two go together."

Leonidas turned away from me and said sharply to Kroton, "Call the troops together."

Kroton and Hamides walked around the camp, calling out in loud voices for all to gather at the king's request. Hoplites in red capes converged on us from all sides. In only a few moments, there was a great crowd encircling us. I kept my eyes downcast. I did not want to see their faces.

"We have a small problem," Leonidas cried out in a great voice. He then motioned towards me.

"This boy has run away from his barracks. He has followed us all the way from home. He has been tracking us, stealing food from our camp, and spying on our movements. He claims he has come to fight the Persians. What say you, Spartans?"

I did not know what to expect. Was he setting me up to be executed, or worse, exiled?

"*Eu-ge! Eu-ge! Eu-ge!*" Their voices thundered around me. Those who arrived at the meeting carrying their shields and spears clashed them together. It was unbelievable. They were cheering. They were voicing their approval of my actions.

"I agree with you, my noble brothers. He has acted as any of us might have at his age: courageous, headstrong, able to live off the land. And yet, he has broken our laws. Without permission he has run away. Without our leave he has followed us here. The law demands he must be punished."

There was a murmuring from the crowd, but I could not tell if they were swayed.

"And what does the law require as punishment?" Leonidas paused, and then answered his own question. "He shall be lashed."

There was another murmuring, and this time I could sense approval. I had been lashed before. I would endure it again.

"Who will whip the boy?" Leonidas called out loudly. "Who will give him his deserved punishment?"

There was more murmuring, yet no one stepped forward. Leonidas looked around, waiting. I wondered why no one volunteered. We Spartans are not polite about such things. It is a simple matter. One is flogged, and then it is over.

"I will," someone called out from the back of the crowd of men. At the sound of his voice, my hair stood on end, and I broke out in a cold sweat. The man worked his way forward. When he came into sight, I hung my head. I could not look him in the eye.

"I'll flog him," he announced loudly. He sounded glad for the chance. "I have a cane and I'm ready." He swung his stick and it whistled through the air.

"Your name?" the king asked.

"Nikandros," he answered. I winced when he said it.

"Boy," Leonidas said. "Over here, to this tree."

The king led me over to a pine tree, the crowd silently giving way for us.

"Put your arms around the tree," the king commanded. "You are a Spartan. There will be no need to tie your hands. You will stay until we are finished with you."

I did as I was ordered. I could feel the sweat running down my sides. I could hear the cane zipping through the air behind me.

"How many, o king?" Nikandros asked. "Twenty? Or forty?" Forty? I had been given six lashes once the year before for getting caught stealing two loaves of bread. One was for me, and the other for my friend Sthenos, who was ill. I was given three for each loaf. I nearly fainted from the pain. How would I survive forty?

"One," the king declared.

"*One?*" Nikandros asked, astonished. "Only *one?* He has broken our laws, broken loyalty to his group. He must be punished. Why, but one? What are we, soft Athenians? He can take it."

"One," Leonidas repeated firmly. "One lash to remind him that he is a Spartan. One lash to his back to remind him that a Spartan never turns his back in battle."

I heard Nikandros snarl behind me, and before I could prepare myself, I felt the cane lash across my bare back. Everything went white for a brief moment before my eyes. I was grateful to have the tree to hold onto. It felt like he had struck me with all his might. Out of the corner of my eye, I saw him throw the cane down onto the ground. It was bent in two. He had broken it on my back with one blow. I took a deep breath and let it out slowly.

He was walking away when Leonidas stopped him, holding him by the arm. He waited a moment while the crowd dispersed. The spectacle was over. Then he spoke softly to him, but they were close enough for me to hear.

"Nikandros, take him with you now. Feed him and care for him. He has broken the law. He has been punished. Now he is one of us."

"You don't intend to let him stay with us?" he asked, astonished.

"It's too late to send him back. He'll be of use to us when things get dicey at the Hot Gates," Leonidas said.

"He's too young to fight," Nikandros protested.

"I never said anything about him fighting, although he may get his share of hand-to-hand before this is over. He has the skills. He's Spartan-raised. Even better, he's Spartan-trained. You may be proud of him. I have the sense that the gods have sent him after us for a reason, though I know not yet what that may be. Now, care for his back and give him some food. Mentor him." When Nikandros did not respond, the king added, "It is family duty."

With these words, Leonidas turned and walked back to his campfire. The man who had whipped me, my own father, stood watching him go. Then he turned to me. "You have disgraced me," he said quietly. "You have shamed our whole family."

I hung my head. I had never considered what I would say to him when we eventually met. I had never thought about it. I only knew that I had to go with him.

Then he shrugged and laughed gruffly. He reached over and ruffled my hair. My heart swelled. "And you have also honored me. Who else has a son who can track the army for five days undetected? Perhaps he's right. You may be of use yet. Now, however, you will be taking away the rations of fighting men. We have little to spare. In this you shame me."

"Father, I shall eat only what I go out and forage from the land. I promise."

He looked at me and then, at last, smiled. "Let that begin tomorrow. Today, you eat with us. You will eat like a Spartan hoplite."

→»⋘←

Nikandros introduced me to his companions, Polydoros, Eunomos, Aristodemos and Cleomenes. They formed a unit and watched one another's back in battle. They stood shoulder to shoulder in the phalanx. They laughed together, bound each other's wounds, shared equally hardship and bounty, and warmed one another at night under their cloaks.

"So this is your youngest," Eunomos said sizing me up. "What year are you?"

"Third year boy," I admitted.

"Well," reckoned Cleomenes. "Still wet behind the ears. Four years away from bearing arms in battle. Who knows? You may get a chance here to test yourself."

"How did you escape?" Polydoros asked. Then he didn't give me a chance to answer. "Never mind. As if we weren't sneaking out of the barracks all the time. It's been so long, I'd nearly forgotten."

"But how could you desert your companions?" Eunomos challenged me. "We swore loyalty to our barrack company. Just as we do to one another in the phalanx line. Have things changed since we were boys?"

"It was hard to decide," I began slowly.

My father's broad hand swung out and slapped me across the head, driving me to my knees.

"Fool of a child!" he spat out. "It's not yours to make decisions. You are a Spartan. You follow orders."

"But, Father," I protested, rubbing my head and staying out of range of another blow. "The oracle. I had to be with you."

All grew silent when I mentioned the oracle.

"It's true, isn't it?" I asked. "Has not Leonidas spoken to you about it?"

"He doesn't need to," Aristodemos said. "We all know about it. What the priestess of Apollo in Delphi declares is no secret. Even if she speaks in riddles."

"But this was not couched in riddles," Polydoros said. "If Sparta is to survive this Persian attack, she can be saved only by the death of a king of the line of Herakles."

"And that's Leonidas," Nikandros added.

"He might not come back," I said.

"We might all not come back," Polydoros said. "That is why he chose us. Look around, boy. Do you see any young men here? He chose us carefully. Each of us leaves behind a son who is old enough to take over the family responsibilities."

"Such as your brother, Anaxandros," my father said.

"Where Leonidas leads, we follow," Eunomos said. "Whom Leonidas fights, we fight. Where Leonidas falls, we fall."

"We are Spartans," Cleomenes said.

Then all together they cried out, raising clutched fists above their heads, "*Eu-ge! Eu-ge! Eu-ge!*"

⇒»≪⇐

The next day as we marched, I slipped away from my father to fulfill my promise. It wasn't long before I returned to him.

"What's that?" Nikandros asked, gesturing at the sack I was carrying. He was walking among his companions, their shields slung over their backs, their long spears resting at a jaunty angle on their shoulders.

"A sack of barley meal. I said I would steal my own food. I have enough to share with the others as well."

Nikandros studied me a moment, and I grew uneasy when he frowned.

"Where did you take it from? Tell me straight, no stories."

"I don't have anything to hide," I said, wondering why he should question me. Stolen goods without getting caught are owned by the thief and we are proud when we succeed. We are trained to succeed. "I took it from the helot camp that follows us. They barely pay attention to their stores."

I was not ready when his long arm swung out and he slapped me across my head. He wore a ring and it hurt when it smacked against my skull.

"Hey, why did you do that?" I protested.

"To knock some sense into your thick head, you fool of a boy. The helot camp that follows us carries our supplies. They feed us every day. You haven't done anything but steal from our own stores."

"Well, how was I to know?" I said, rubbing my head. "Back in Sparta, we always steal from the helots."

"Well, out here, little one, if you want to be of help, you have to find someone else to steal from."

"I will," I said firmly. I looked at the bag of meal in my hands. "What should I do with this? Take it back?"

"You *are* a cabbage head. And risk a beating? I'll give it back to them when they bring our evening meal."

I shrugged my shoulders. I was learning many lessons out here on the campaign trail.

Suddenly, there was a commotion from further ahead in our column. Word of some event was being passed along.

"Thespians! Many hundreds."

"Who are the Thespians?" I asked.

"Citizens of Thespiae, no doubt," my father said with a shrug.

"I mean, friend or foe?"

"Judging that we haven't been called into battle position, I would say it's still up in the air. Come on. If we hurry, we can get close enough to hear what's going on." And he broke into a trot. I was impressed that after a day of marching, he still could trot carrying his shield and spear. He seemed so immensely strong to me. Would I ever be that strong?

We had been walking close to the head of the column and soon came to a knot of hoplites around Leonidas. He was talking to another Greek. I now understood what Kroton had meant the day before. This stranger—although he spoke Greek, it sounded different from our own tongue. It had a strong flavor of something unfamiliar and foreign, yet was still within my reach to understand. Behind and around him stood his contingent of soldiers. They were dressed similarly to our hoplites, yet had a style all their own. They looked more pieced together than our hoplites. Shields weren't matching, nor were their helmets.

"...great joy to see Spartans," the man was saying.

"I am Leonidas." We'd arrived in time for introductions.

"Well, the king himself. This gets better and better. How many do you bring?"

"Three hundred."

"But three hundred?" he exclaimed. "We are more than twice your number."

"That may be," Leonidas spoke deliberately. "But my three hundred are Spartans."

The Greek laughed. "And we are Thespians. I am Demophilos. We are headed to the Hot Gates."

"And so are we. Let us throw our lot together."

"We are surprised to see you. We had heard that the Spartans were not leaving Pelops' Isle."

"You heard correctly. Our Ephors were hesitant to send any force at all. We are still in the midst of celebrating the festival of Karneia. Our priests were not happy with the position of the Pleiades. Also, the moon was not propitious for leaving on a campaign. Besides, our Ephors are convinced we can hold off the Persians at the Isthmus, at Corinth."

"Yet you are here."

"I reckon that if the Persians break past the Isthmus, what is left to keep them from our front doors? We need the Athenians to stop them before they reach the Isthmus, as they did once before at Marathon. And the Athenians need us to slow the Persians down so they can get ready. I figure we can handle that."

"But with so few."

"Yes, we are few, but every one a Spartan."

"So you said before. But what difference can that make?" Demophilos challenged.

Leonidas studied the Thespian troops a moment. He singled one out.

"You there, what do you do?"

"I'm a stone carver," he said proudly. Leonidas pointed at another.

"And you? What is your training?"

"I'm a weaver."

"And you?"

"I tend my farm."

Then Leonidas turned to the men around him. He slapped the man beside him on the chest with the back of his hand.

"What are you trained to do, Archidamos?"

"Fight!" he said without hesitation.

Leonidas turned to another. "And you, Eurykrates?"

"Fight!"

"And what about you, Nikandros?" he asked, looking at my father.

"Fight!" he shouted even louder than the others.

Leonidas returned his gaze to Demophilos.

"Any other questions?"

Demophilos was obviously enjoying himself. He had a smile beneath his shaggy beard.

"Well, we look forward to seeing if your reputation walks with you. Just know, we are not alone. Townsmen from all around will be joining us: Phocians and Locrians. Our scouts have reported a contingent of Corinthians and Thebans will soon arrive. We will number several thousand."

"Then the Persians shall have no lack of entertainment with us."

"If we can convince the others to stick around," Demophilos said.

"Do you expect them to run when they see the Persians?"

"A touch of fear goes a long way in battle. No, it is worse than that. Xerxes sent his emissaries to every city. He demanded we offer up earth and water as a sign of obedience to the king."

Leonidas laughed roughly. "We also had a visit from his emissaries. We gave them what they asked for." All Sparta knew what happened on the day that richly dressed Persians bedecked with gold chain and jewels arrived and declared Sparta a vassal to Xerxes' empire. Leonidas himself led them out to the edge of the city where there is a great pit that we use as a common privy. He had the emissaries thrown in, declaring, "There is your earth. There is your water. Take these gifts back to your king with our respects."

Demophilos laughed. "All Greece has heard about the homage Sparta paid to Persia. Yet others were not so courageous. Or so straightforward."

"So what is the problem?" Leonidas asked.

"He sends his emissaries back to those who refused the first time. He now offers us gold if we betray our people and our land. He is clever like a snake. If he cannot make us bow in fear, he tries to buy us. He has found the true weakness of the Greeks. Many have already fallen to this treachery before a single arrow has been shot. Yet I understand their motives. It is not only the gold.

Fear plays its part as well. They say that Xerxes brings an army that will cover the land like ants."

"We need not worry on either account. Spartans care little for money."

It was true what he said. Our laws forbid us from possessing any. But who cares? We have what we need without money.

"And the other?" Demophilos asked.

"We have no fear of ants. We crush them beneath our feet."

"So we shall see," Demophilos said, shrugging his shoulders. He looked up at the sky. "Day is waning. My scouts report that an hour from here is a well-watered and sheltered place to camp. We are headed there to spend the night."

"Then we shall camp beside you," Leonidas replied.

"What an honor," Demophilos said grimly.

Over the next few days, our column swelled as more and more Greeks joined in our march. I no longer had to steal from the helots. There were plenty of other unsuspecting camps into which I could sneak. I had learned my lessons well. I was able to bring more than a few treats back to my father's companions. They accepted me as one of their own. Even Father frowned less and less when he saw me.

One evening as we took our rest, Polydoros returned excitedly.

"It's been decided," he declared.

"What?"

"Leonidas. He's been chosen by the other Greek city-states to lead us all into battle. I was present at the council. We are nearly four thousand now."

"If I know Leonidas," Cleomenes said, "he will keep the others in reserve. It will fall to us to hold the Gates."

"Who else?" exclaimed Aristodemos. "From what I've seen, they are nothing but a rag-tag collection of hoplites. Hardly a properly equipped man among them."

"It's as if we would send the *perioikoi* to battle, our merchants and artisans," Polydoros said with scorn in his voice. "It's an insult they call themselves hoplites."

"How long before we come to the Gates?" my father asked.

"Tomorrow eve," Polydoros reported. "If the scouts are to be trusted."

"We'll be in the vanguard after this," Cleomenes said. "Let the rest straggle behind. Mark my word, we'll make double time and be there before Helios begins his descent."

"Sparta!" Aristodemos exclaimed.

"Sparta!" the rest cried out together.

Cleomenes was right. Leonidas had us roused the moment it was light enough to see the difference between one face and the next. He declared we would eat with our first break. Then we set off at a trot. I marveled at the hoplites around me. Carrying their shields and spears, they held a pace that challenged me over time, and I was not carrying anything. By the time the sun was shining down on us, I was in a full sweat. There was not a word of complaint from around me. Just the pounding of feet and the rattle of armor.

As the morning wore on, the terrain around us changed dramatically. The mountains to the west grew higher and closer. The plains to the east ended abruptly showing a wedge of distant water, which looked to be a spur of an inlet. Beyond the water I could clearly see the mountainous coast on the far side. Then I lost track of time and gave up all thought of rest and food. We were on a Spartan march, and it was not up to us to question its duration.

We turned around a bend, and the high cliffs closed in around us. Before us was a narrow passage between them into the mountain. Our company was finally called to halt. Only then did I see the effects of the exertion on the hoplites. All were breathing hard. Some were bent over, their hands resting on their knees. I watched a few walk off to the side and throw up.

Leonidas appeared among us. He, too, was breathing hard, his face streaked with sweat. Yet his eyes had a gleam in them that betrayed his excitement.

"Behold!" he called out in a loud voice. "The Hot Gates! We have arrived. Prepare to make camp."

While some of the men leaned in exhaustion against the stone walls of the mountain, others began to mill about, setting their shields down, looking around. I went up to Nikandros.

"Father, why is it called the Hot Gates? Because there will be a fight here?"

He waved me off with his hand. "Not now." He looked spent. He was gently touching his arm where the edge of his shield had rubbed the skin raw.

I walked off, eager to explore. Since Leonidas had not forbidden it, I walked beyond where we stopped and entered the cleft between the cliffs. Immediately I noticed an odd, pungent smell. Smoke hung in the air in that narrow place. It felt inhabited, but not by mortals. I wondered with a thrill if I had stumbled on the dwelling of some mountain nymph or satyr. I loudly spoke propitiating words that they welcome me. I wished to find running water to wash my hands and seal my prayer. The last thing I needed was to be put under a spell from those semi-divine beings that we share the earth with.

Ahead of me the passage opened up wider and sunlight slanted in from fissures in the roof. Here the smoke I had seen upon entering hung thickly. I stopped in my tracks. I could hear the sound of dripping water.

By now the strange smell had grown even more intense. I was thirsty from our long march, and I let my ears lead me to the water. There was a low break in the cliff wall at one place, in the shape of a large triangle. It was from inside there that the sound of water was coming. I got down on my knees and peered inside. My nostrils flared at the unfamiliar smell. My face felt wet. I realized it was not smoke hovering in the air, but mist! I felt heat rising from the water warming my face, and I concluded that I had been a second time mistaken. It was not mist in the air, but steam.

I reached out my hand to feel what my eyes in the dark could not see. I pulled it back immediately. Something had burned my fingers! Yet now I could tell that my hand was wet. I had placed my hand in scalding water. Hot Gates. Of course. Here was a place of thermal pools. I had heard of such things, but we had none near Sparta. I laughed with pleasure. Our men will delight in easing their aching muscles in these healing waters.

I spoke a brief prayer to the nymph of the pools and quickly dipped my fingertips into the hot water to seal my words.

I was about to turn back, but my curiosity drew me on. I wanted to see where this narrow passage led. The way remained constricted until it suddenly opened up and I walked out into the space beyond.

To my right, the broad ocean spread out. I had long heard tales of the sea, but this was the first time I had ever stood and gazed at its immensity. Gulls circled in the air, and their cries mixed with the breaking of the waves below the high cliffs. I was excited by the sounds and the smells.

To my left the mountain rose up high overhead. From there to the cliffs overlooking the sea was a span about fifty feet wide. Across this stood the remains of a wall. It looked like, at some time, the locals had wanted to fortify this spot, to make it as narrow as possible, to prevent an armed force from passing.

I stood there in the full sunlight and breathed in deeply the smell of the ocean. I wanted to remember this moment forever. Only then did I look up and see that before me stretched long widening plains where the mountains gradually gave way. What I saw there took my breath away.

The broad, level land, from ocean spur to receding mountains, was completely covered. Everywhere I looked, all I could see was in movement. Columns and rows of soldiers stretched endlessly, the sun glancing off their helmets and shields. It was bizarre and amazing. Before me marched an army so immense that it was true what Demophilos had said. They covered the land like ants. I could only stand and gape.

Then to my horror, I realized that this whole mass of humanity was moving directly towards the spot upon which I stood. A panic seized me. I had to tell the king.

"Behold the might of Persia," a deep voice spoke beside me. I nearly jumped out of my skin. I whirled around. Half a step behind me stood Leonidas.

"It seems we've come none too soon," he said.

"Shall I run and call the hoplites?" I asked breathlessly, holding back my panic.

"No need. They're on their way," he said. He did not look particularly alarmed.

"But they could be here any moment," I said, waving my arms towards the Persian forces.

"I'm not so sure," he said lazily. "Looks like they're making camp for the night. The most we'll see is a scout or two."

I stared out into the plains. I did not know so many people existed in the whole world as marched in the plains before us.

"These are more Persians than all of Greece," I said with wonderment.

"Don't be deceived, boy. What you see is the empire of Persia. From every land that accepts Xerxes as their king, he demands more than earth and water. He requires that they provide him an army. Medes, Babylonians, Phrygians—the list is as long as your imagination— Lydians, Scythians, Thracians, Egyptians and, yes, even

Greeks. Those are not fighters down there. No more than the farmers, blacksmiths, potters and merchants who make up the Thespian army."

"Yet they are so many."

"That's the reason why we're here, boy," Leonidas said slowly. "This spot is one of several choke points in Greece. The mountains have long been our defense against invasion from the north. In order for them to go any further south by land, they have to pass through these narrows. With my three hundred alone we can hold this place a long time. That is what the Athenians are counting on. To buy them some time. Let's see how much we can give them."

Several other Spartans had now joined us.

"There they are," said one. "Marvelous."

"They will give us good sport," said another.

"What an ideal place to hold."

"Let's make it even better," Leonidas spoke loudly. "This wall was a good idea, but it has seen better days. Men, set to and repair it. I want it twice its height. And extend it all the way to the edge of the cliffs. It will give us good backing and keep them from getting around behind us. And with a wall behind us, they can push us back only so far. And push us they will."

Many hands set to work. They were cheerful as they went about finding stones and clearing the path in front of the passageway.

"Hey," called Leonidas. "Wasn't there a stone mason among those Thespians? Boy, see if they've arrived yet and fetch him here. Tell him to bring his tools and anyone else who understands stone. We have need of handworkers skilled in wall building.

I didn't need to be told twice. Off I ran to find the Thespians and bring the workers the king desired.

⇢⟫⟪⇠

By evening, the rebuilding of the wall was well underway. Many Thespians has come at my calling and taken over working on the wall. Out in the plains, although there was still a considerable amount of movement, they no longer pressed forward. Based on the smoke, many campfires were burning.

"They are resting for the night," Aristodemos commented to me. "Before long we should see their scouts, testing if they will meet any resistance when they want to move through tomorrow."

The Spartan hoplites had cleared away all debris and loose stones from the area before the wall. They had taken over this space and were exercising and stretching. Spartan muscles, in order to remain supple and strong, need taking caring of. Some of the men had unbound their long braids. They were combing and oiling their hair. I knew what this meant. These men expected that

they might die the next day in battle. We Spartans make ourselves beautiful to go and meet death.

Several looked up abruptly. The sound of hoof-beats was approaching. No one looked alarmed or ran to take up arms. They continued exercising and combing, watching the road with curiosity.

Around a bend in the road came three riders. They slowed their pace when they saw us gathered there. They continued to advance, but came cautiously. Leonidas went out to meet them. He, too, had been exercising, and he stood there naked, calm and unafraid, streaked with sweat, looking like Father Zeus on a visit to walk upon Mother Gaia and meddle in the affairs of mortals. He raised his hand in greeting. Or perhaps to gesture they come no nearer.

When the riders were a stone's throw away, they reined in their horses. Two had unusual features and were were dressed in strange garb. They were clearly barbarians. The third was dressed in Greek fashion. He leaned over and spoke to the others. They studied us keenly.

"Normally, I would offer hospitality," Leonidas called out. "But seeing you come armed, you may not pass."

"Ah, a Spartan god, far from home," the Greek grunted. He had a strange way of speaking.

"Ah, an Ionian traitor," Leonidas responded. "Also far from home."

"Translator," he corrected. "I have no love for these Persians, but their numbers are very persuasive, in case you haven't noticed."

"Still, you may not pass," Leonidas said.

"And you think to hold this place with so few, against *them*?" and he turned in his saddle to gesture at the distant plains covered by the Persian army.

"That we shall leave to the gods to decide," Leonidas replied.

"Well, we've seen what we've come to see. Until the morning." The Greek spoke again to his two companions. They stared for a few moments longer at the men before them, and then the three rode away. Leonidas watched them go and then returned to his exercises.

⇒⟫⟪⇐

By first light the next morning, the Spartans were lined up in front of the wall, fed, limber and in full armor. Leonidas had asked the Thespians under Demophilos to wait as reserves in the passageway behind the wall. He ordered the rest of the Greek troops to remain at the southern entrance to the passage. The Spartans, he told them, would take the brunt of the attack. When they saw the immensity of the Persian camp, no one quarreled with him.

My father was just telling me to go stand with the Corinthians. I was arguing with him that I didn't want to leave.

"These are not maneuvers," he insisted. "They will kill you in an instant."

"I won't go," I stood my ground. "I've come to be part of this."

Just then Leonidas was passing by. He paused and listened a moment to our argument. "I have an idea," he said, interrupting. We both looked up. "I've noticed that there is a natural alcove behind the rocks above the gate. It is well protected in front. It is also under an outcropping, so, should they shoot arrows, he will be covered from above as well. I'd like him up there."

"Whatever for?" demanded my father.

"One never knows. Perhaps an extra pair of Spartan eyes will come in handy."

"And what if he see me fall?" Nikandros asked his king, obviously distressed.

"Then make sure you do not," was his calm response.

It was settled. With the king's leave, I climbed the rock wall to the perch above. As I was climbing, I overheard Kroton say to Leonidas, "If he can get up there, so can a Persian."

"All the more reason to have a Spartan there first."

He took a lance and called to me. "Here, boy, take this." He tossed it up to me.

"What do you want me to do with this?" I asked, perplexed.

"Any Persian comes your way, skewer him."

"With pleasure!" I called down.

I had barely settled myself when I heard the sound of horses approaching. I looked up and realized I could see further around the bend than from the ground.

"Who comes, boy?" Leonidas called to me.

"It's the Ionian again," I reported. "And he comes with five barbarians. They are more richly dressed than the two from yesterday."

"They come to talk," Leonidas commented to his men. "I will go meet them." He took off his helmet and laid aside his shield and spear. He walked into the open space before his men.

The six horsemen rode into the clearing and stopped their mounts several paces in front of Leonidas. The Ionian Greek turned in his saddle and spoke with the rider beside him. The Persian wore a large turban with a jewel set at his forehead. His expression was severe. He wore a cape and his legs were wrapped with colorful cloth. I had never seen anything like that before. All at the same time, he looked grand, noble and absurd. He raised himself in the stirrups and began to speak. I could not understand a word he was saying. Leonidas waited patiently until he was finished. When the Persian settled himself back in his saddle, Leonidas addressed the Greek.

"Translate, Ionian."

"He is a *satrap*, a governor of vast territories in Persia. Never mind his name, you couldn't pronounce it anyway. He wants you to know that he governs a land greater than all of Greece."

"I am unimpressed," Leonidas said.

"He wants you to know that the great Xerxes, king of kings, recognizes your bravery. Yet he asks, why throw away such courage? You see the size of his forces. You know that he will send against you wave upon wave of spearmen and swordsmen, and you will quickly be overcome as the frothy waves overcome the naked shore."

"Spare me the poetry," Leonidas interrupted. "The great sea sends wave upon wave towards the shore, yet the rocks still stand. So shall we."

The Persian satrap spoke hurriedly to the Ionian. The Ionian, motioning to the sea, answered. I reckoned he was translating what Leonidas had said.

"The great Xerxes wishes to offer you a choice," the Ionian continued. "If you will lay down your arms, he will raise you to be king."

"I already am a king," Leonidas said with a shrug.

"The Great Xerxes will make you king over all of Greece. Such courage as yours deserves a great reward."

"And what are his conditions, should I accept such a generous offer?" Leonidas asked.

"The only requirement is to bow down to Xerxes and accept him as your supreme ruler. It is that simple, Spartan. Consider well your choices."

Leonidas seemed to ponder the words of the Ionian. He gazed out over the sea. He turned a moment and glanced at the wall, the opening to the passage, at his men lined up in battle order. His eyes surveyed the mountain rising beside them. His eyes rested a moment on me, sending a thrill through my whole body. Then he looked up at the sky above.

"May the Olympians be my witness," he pronounced loudly. "Go and tell Xerxes that if he knew what is good in life, he would not wish for foreign things, but be content with his own. I am a king over the best and the finest. For me, I know it would be better to die for a free Sparta than to be king over all of Greece if they be but slaves and vassals to a foreign power."

"*Eu-ge!*" exploded the Spartans in approval of his words, clashing their spears against their shields.

"You are a fool, Spartan," the Ionian spit back. "There is no escape but death. Swordsmen will swarm over the ground like ants. Arrows will fly so thickly through the air that they will blot out the sun." He flourished his arm in a great arc to include the whole sky.

"All the better, Ionian," a voice shouted from the line of Spartans. "Then we shall fight in the shade."

Laughter at this comment rose up from the ranks.

"Spartan," said the Ionian. "Here is your last chance. Give up your arms."

Leonidas glanced over his shoulder to the left and to the right at the three hundred hoplites behind him. Then he looked at the Ionian and his words flew sharply like an arrow loosed from the bow.

"Come and take them."

"*Eu-ge! Eu-ge! Eu-ge!*" shouted the Spartans, clashing their spears against their shields. Leonidas turned on his heel and walked back to his men. He put on his helmet, slipped his arm into his shield, and picked up his spear.

The six horsemen wheeled their mounts and galloped away.

"Spartans!" he yelled. "Phalanx order. Give no quarter. Leave none standing. Wounded or tired, rotate to the rear, rest and rejoin."

We didn't have long to wait. From down in the plains trumpets blared. Nearer by, a shout from countless voices went up. I was the first to see them.

"They're coming," I yelled down. "They fill the road!"

Now we could hear the pounding of their feet and the rattling of their shields against their short swords. As soon as they rounded the bend and saw the line of the phalanx, they let out a loud shout. At the same moment, the phalanx did the same. The line of Persians charged up against the shields of the Spartans. The line of shields faltered and was pushed back several feet, yet it held.

The hoplites in the first line hunkered behind their shields and dug in their heels. Over their shoulders, the second and third lines stretched out their long spears and stabbed at the Persians in the front. The Persians wore leathern helmets, but their armor looked to be made of cane. Their shields were of a similar substance woven together. It was easy for the Spartan iron spear points to penetrate the feeble shields and armor of the charging forces. The short swords of the Persians found no one to stab or slash. They were faced with a wall of shields. To make their predicament more difficult, they were pushed from behind, right onto the waiting spears of the Spartans.

I watched my father and his companions in the second row of shields. They thrust their spears against the attacking force and sharply pulled them back, and a moment later, locating a new target, thrust again. With every thrust a Persian fell.

The dead piled up. As the pile grew at their feet, the oncoming Persians climbed over them. Many tried to leap up over the line of shields, only to impale themselves on the Spartan spears. This went on for some time until the mound of the dead and wounded before the hoplites was so great that the Persians could no longer reach them.

Several horns blew loudly, and suddenly the Persians retreated.

"Regroup!" Leonidas commanded. "Injured, rotate to the back! Shields at the ready!"

There was some movement along the lines as a few men wormed their way back and others took their places in front.

Several voices suddenly shouted, "Tortoise!" Immediately, all the shields locked together on the sides and over their heads like the armor of a giant tortoise. I knew what that command meant. I pressed myself against the rock wall.

A hail of arrows fell upon us. I could hear many of them striking the metal shields. I heard them tickering off the stones above and around me. I was able to press myself into a crease in the rock where I was crouching and keep out of harm's way.

After what seemed like half a dozen breaths, the arrows stopped and the hoplites slowly emerged. Their shields were peppered with arrows, so the tortoise now looked like a giant hedgehog. The rain of arrows did not seem to have injured anyone. It had, however, served to kill any wounded Persian who had escaped death at the hands of the Greeks.

"Ah, blessed shade," a voice called out. There were guffaws of laughter.

"Thespians! To work!" Leonidas yelled.

It must have been a pre-arranged plan. While the Spartan hoplites held their position, water skins were hastily passed around. While they refreshed themselves,

Thespians poured out from behind the wall and dragged the bodies of the dead Persians off to the side of the road. They pushed them off the cliffs and into the sea below.

"Keep watch!" Leonidas called up to me. "Give warning!"

I knew my job was to give the Thespians a chance to escape behind the Spartan phalanx before the next attack came. They were just clearing away the last bodies when the Persians returned.

"Make ready!" I called down. "They fill the road!"

Just as before, the next onslaught came. They ran, they yelled, they threw themselves against the wall of Spartan shields. The press from behind pushed their companions onto our waiting spear points. The Spartans of the second row had little more to do than hold their spears out firmly. Once again, the dead piled up. When the wall of the dead grew so great that the Persians could no longer reach the line of shields, they retreated once again.

A second time a rain of arrows pelted the tortoise. When it was finished, out came the Thespians and cleared away the dead. Hardly had they finished, and the Persians attacked again. This was repeated over and over again during the long day. I lost track of how many times the Persian forces threw themselves to their deaths against the phalanx.

The outcome of this spectacle was so predictable that I grew weary of watching. The only thing that changed was that the road grew muddy with blood. When I looked out to sea, I could see countless bodies floating on the billows.

Towards afternoon, I must have dozed off. Watching the fighting, my eyes had grown so heavy that I wanted to close them only for a moment. Above the din and clash of battle, I was roused by someone sharply calling my name.

"Agis! Awaken! *Agis!!*"

I opened my eyes to see a Persian climbing up to where I was sitting. He was only a few feet below me, his long knife in one hand as he tried to keep himself from falling. He had a bow and quiver slung over his shoulder, and my immediate thought was that he wanted my perch to rain arrows down on the Spartans. My lance was in my hand, and, without thinking, I turned it towards the oncoming Persian and thrust it through his neck. His eyes grew wide and his face was contorted with pain. He struck his knife feebly against the haft of the lance and, dragging it with him, tumbled to the ground below.

I looked down to see how the battle was going. My eyes were drawn to the back of the phalanx. My father stood in the last line, staring up at me. When he saw that I was unharmed, he turned his attention back to the battle.

It had been a near call. I had no idea how one of the Persians could have gotten by the phalanx to climb up the hillside. I wondered if he had crawled underneath the line of shields. However he did it, I realized I had to stay alert if I were to stay alive.

The rest of the day passed slowly. I thought that the men in the phalanx must be exhausted, but then I realized they were able to fight in shifts. They fought in this way until nightfall. Only then did the Persians cease their attack.

Once it was clear that the Persians had given up for the day, the phalanx disbanded and moved into the passageway. I watched the Theban force move forward. They must have drawn the night watch, to give the Spartans time to rest and sleep.

I clambered down from my perch. My father was waiting for me. I saw that Leonidas was standing beside him.

"He's looking no worse for wear," Leonidas said. "And he's killed his first man in battle."

"He fell asleep," my father said severely.

"Monotonous work it was," Leonidas said with a shrug.

"Were any of our men killed?" I asked.

"None," he said with satisfaction. "A few wounds to bind, but nothing serious. As I told you, we faced only farmers and handworkers. I am worried about one thing, though."

"What is that?" Nikandros asked.

"How that Persian slipped by us." He looked up the side of the rock cliff. "It made me wonder if there's a way over this mountain. If they find a way to come in behind us, it will be our last battle."

"Let's hope the Persians don't think of it," my father said.

"And yet, we have to expect they will. I think I'll send the Phocians out to watch our back. They know the mountain paths and where to watch."

That night, as tired as they were, my father's companions were in good cheer.

"I've never been in such a battle," Polydoros said. "They threw themselves right onto our spears."

"Little choice they had," said Aristodemos. "Did you not see the captains behind them with their whips?"

It was true. From midday on, the Persian attack had been driven from behind by a row of men whipping the soldiers forward.

"We won't be so lucky tomorrow," Cleomenes said.

"How do you mean?" my father asked.

"These were untrained soldiers," he said. "Similar to the Phocians and Locrians Leonidas won't let into the battle. Xerxes imagined he would find only local townsmen here and the sheer number of his soldiers would overwhelm them. I'm willing to wager that tomorrow Xerxes will send against us his personal bodyguard, the Immortals."

"The Immortals?" Eunomos exclaimed. "Are they gods?"

"Only in number," Cleomenes explained. "Rumor is that there are ten thousand of them. When one falls, he is replaced by the next morning, so the number is never diminished."

"Well, tomorrow Xerxes will have many to replace," Aristodemos said.

"We'll see," Cleomenes said. "I'm certain the Immortals have been trained to fight. And I expect they'll be wearing real armor."

"Then we'd best get our rest," Polydoros said. "Time to turn in."

Without another word, we all lay down and went to sleep.

⇒⟫⟪⇐

In the pre-dawn darkness the phalanx got in place.

"Any activity?" I heard Leonidas ask the Theban captain as they filed into the passageway.

"All night. They came in small bands of five or ten in the dark, testing if our guard was down."

"Did they give you any trouble?"

"I kept a patrol in the deepest shadows along the road. As soon as a raiding party passed them, they sprang out and skewered them from behind."

"What did you do with the bodies?"

"We left them piled neatly along the road to greet the Persians as they come this morning, so they will know what's waiting for them."

"Rest well," Leonidas said. "And help watch the paths behind us coming out of the mountains. The Persians will be looking for a way around."

I climbed up again to my lookout perch. This day, Leonidas tossed up two lances.

"I wouldn't want you to be left empty-handed again," he called up. "Try to hang onto them this time."

Day approached, and it was not long before I heard the blasts of many horns and the beating of drums. The mountain I leaned against seemed to tremble and vibrate. Around the bend I saw the approaching troops.

"They come! They come!" I called down.

In the dim light, they looked fearsome. It was true what Cleomenes had said. These were not the troops from the day before. They came walking in ranks, orderly and deliberate. These must be the Immortals. They were dressed in black and I could hear the unmistakable clanking of armor.

I looked down at the phalanx and, to my astonishment, saw it was breaking apart. The front line had separated from the rest of the unit and was walking forward. I could not comprehend what they were doing. It was certain death to separate from the rest of their comrades.

Their line was just wide enough to span the road. They were a good fifty paces ahead of the body of the phalanx. They stood there, their shields over-lapping, their spears extended. What sort of suicide was Leonidas leading them into?

As soon as the Immortals saw the single line of hoplites, they let out a war cry and charged. The Spartan line held, but the battle was immediate and fierce. There was no second line behind them to reach over their shoulders and stab. They had to hold the line and fight at the same time. It was inevitable that they could not hold for long against the mass of Immortals pressing upon them.

Leonidas himself shouted a signal. As one man, the line turned in unison and fled. I was aghast. Spartans never turn their backs in battle, never flee. I pinched myself. Was I caught in some sort of nightmare?

The Immortals saw their advantage, cried victory, and gave pursuit. With a shudder, I expected next to see the whole phalanx crumble. Suddenly, the fleeing line of hoplites, with the same precision as they had fled, pivoted on a foot, turned and extended their spears. The charging line of Immortals could not stop so suddenly and impaled themselves on the waiting spear points.

Seeing what had happened so easily to their brethren, the Immortals behind them paused.

The line of hoplites had counted on this hesitation. They melted away, back to the phalanx, and behind them stood a new line of hoplites, shields interlocked, spears extended. They charged into the Immortals. The Persians were taken off-guard to have fresh men facing them. The hand-to-hand drove them back several feet and many fell. Then they regrouped and surged forward again.

After several minutes of fighting, the line of hoplites again turned as one man and fled. The Immortals who were now in front had no idea what had happened to the first lines to fall and so also fell into the trap. They pursued. As soon as the Spartans turned around again, the Persians were impaled on the hoplites' waiting spears. Then the line of Spartans dissolved as before, revealing a new line, fresh and eager to give battle.

Every time a new line came forward, it drove back the mass of Immortals waiting for their turn to fight on the front line. The dead and wounded were beginning to pile up in the space between the phalanx and the line of Spartan hoplites who had gone out to engage the Immortals. Then the Thespians rushed out, dispatched the dying and dragged away the dead, pushing them over the cliff into the sea below. Just as they finished, the signal was given, and the line of Spartans retreated.

This was repeated throughout the morning. By the time the original line returned to the front, they were rested and ready for another run. The Immortals, blocking their own view of what was going on because the road was so narrow, fell into the trap every time.

This was much riskier work than the day before, and I saw several hoplites take serious wounds. Coming out into the open to fight exposed them more and more. As the day wore on and their own exhaustion began to show, Persians were able to slip behind the line and either attack the waiting phalanx, which was foolish, or worse, turn and wound a Spartan from behind.

At one point, I saw Aristodemos led off the field, leaning on Polydoros. He held a hand to his face, and there was blood streaming down his cheek. I tried to track my father, but there was so much going on, I frequently lost sight of him.

At one point, Leonidas pulled back all of his lines and let the phalanx stand as one unit. The Immortals, always fresh, surged against them. But the Spartans were tired from the day before, and I saw several fall. Regardless, the wall of dead Persians grew again, until their warriors could no longer reach the front line of shields. They retreated, giving our men a rest and the Thespians a chance to clear the battlefield.

I took this chance to come down from my perch to relieve myself. Then I searched the faces of the men milling about, looking for my father or one of his companions. Finally I found Polydoros.

"How is Aristodemos?" I asked.

"He's lost an eye. Otherwise no worse. Leonidas has ordered him to stay out of the battle for now."

"Have you seen my father?"

"The last I saw Nikandros, he was helping the Thespians dispatch the wounded Persians."

I walked quickly onto the battleground. There was no telling how long we had until the next attack. I saw him, short sword in hand. He had seen me and was slowly walking towards me. His arms were streaked with blood, and he looked tired.

"Go back!" he called out, gesturing with his sword. "Get back to your perch!"

I looked at him and felt my hair stand on end. I did not stop to think and I had no time for words. I ran towards him as fast as I could. I dropped one of my two lances and flung the other straight at him.

My father's eyes grew large as he watched me attack him, and wordlessly, he threw himself to the ground. The lance passed through the spot where he had stood a moment before and pierced the throat of the Persian with raised sword who had been about to run it through my father's back. He must have feigned dead and was going to take this chance to ambush one of the Greeks. He fell with a clatter of arms beside my father. Nikandros turned and finished him off with his sword.

He rose from the ground and walked over to me, placing his hand on my shoulder. He had a grim look in his eyes.

"Let no man doubt your courage," he said. "But for a moment, I thought you had gone crazy."

"I did not know what else to do," I said. "And words would not come."

"You found the right action. You learned today how to watch a man's back. Now, for my sake, return to the safety of your perch."

With my second lance again in hand, I clambered up to my lookout. I peered down the road and barely had time to yell down, "They return!" before the Persians appeared around the bend.

The rest of the day passed in constant battle. Sometimes the phalanx stood its ground, at other times, they sent out a single line to lay a trap for the Persians. Wave after wave, the Immortals came against us. Facing these trained soldiers, some Spartans fell, yet I knew Xerxes would be furious to have to replace so many of his elite group, and this gave me grim pleasure.

When evening came, the fighting ended as it had the day before. The Persians retreated, leaving their dead behind. The Spartan phalanx filed slowly into the passageway, and the Thebans came to take their place and hold the entrance to the Hot Gates.

I walked among the men. They were not so high-spirited as the day before. I could sense their exhaustion. They barely spoke among themselves. Some of their spears were broken, their hafts hacked in two. They lay useless and scattered. Their shields were dented and broken, some so badly that they were beyond use. Swords were nicked, edges dulled and several broken. Helots walked around the field, looking for weapons they could repair or replace. Other helots mingled with the men, bringing food and tending to the wounded. I found my father and his companions. Cleomenes was having his forearm bandaged.

"A mere scratch," he protested, although the blood was already soaking through the bandaging.

Polydoros showed me his right hand. His small finger was reduced to a bloody stump. The finger next to it was missing the last digit.

"His blade struck me on the pommel," he explained and shrugged his shoulders. "I can still grip it, though."

My father had long, ugly scratches on his arm. "He tried to bite me, too," he said. "So I made him eat my blade instead."

Aristodemos was the worst wounded. "My helmet had been knocked back, and then he slashed me across the face with his sword." He had lost one eye, and the other was swollen and difficult for him to see out of.

Eunomos, they told me, had been struck in the neck by an arrow that the Persians had begun shooting over the line of fighting into the phalanx behind.

"He lies with the other dead in the passageway, covered by his shield," Cleomenes explained.

The mood of the companions, having lost one of their own, was somber.

As we sat in silence and ate, a commotion arose around us. The men reached for their weapons and stood, ready to fend off a surprise attack from the Persians. Then we heard what it was about. Leonidas was calling all the Greeks to a council.

"What do you think it could be?" I asked Cleomenes as we walked towards the open space at the opposite end of the passageway. I noticed he was limping and that his foot was wrapped up.

"A Persian lance," he commented. "I'll be fine by morning."

I kept him company as the others rushed past us.

"Whatever Leonidas wants, it's no good news if he wants to speak with all of us."

Leonidas was already speaking to those assembled when we arrived. "...Phocians fled when they saw them," he was saying. "Probably for the best. I think we have at least until morning."

"What do you propose?" a chieftain asked.

"My Spartans and I will remain to hold the pass. This will give the rest of the Greek forces a chance to escape."

"But they will surround you! You'll be cut to pieces!"

"Better than all of us getting cut to pieces. You are free to choose. I suggest you leave, warn others and fight another day."

Cleomenes tugged at Polydoros' tunic.

"What did we miss?" he whispered.

"We are betrayed. The Persians have found a path over the mountain. A large force will be coming down in the morning. Must have been a Greek who showed them the way. Xerxes probably offered him, too, to be king over all of Greece. "

There was a lot of movement around us. Greek commanders were calling out orders to their men.

"Spartans!" It was the voice of Leonidas. "Gather to me!"

When we stood around him in a great ring many men deep, he addressed us.

"Spartans, you've heard what I've offered the other Greeks. My offer is the same to you. I remain to fulfill the oracle. Yet it said nothing of your sacrifice. You are free to stay or go. What say you, Spartans?"

"*Eu-ge! Eu-ge! Eu-ge!*" Their war cry echoed off the mountain walls.

"We follow where our king leads!" a voice called out.

"Then go to your rest. Make yourselves beautiful, for tomorrow we go to meet our ancestors."

As the Spartans wandered back to their camps, Demophilos, the leader of the Thespians, walked up to Leonidas.

"My men and I will remain by your side," he said. "Most everyone who can carry arms is here, anyway. We can better defend Thespiae united with you than standing alone."

"Then have your men rest and be ready in the morning," Leonidas said. He then turned and saw me. "For you, lad, I have a special mission."

"I am not afraid," I said, my voice shaking.

"That you have already proven. Find Aristodemos and return to me with him."

I did not have to look far. Polydoros was leading him back to our camp. The swelling had worsened, and he could see very little now. He placed his hand on my shoulder and let me lead him back to Leonidas.

"Kinsman," Leonidas said when he saw him, "I have heard of your wound."

"It will clear by morning," Aristodemos said. "And my arms are still strong."

"And are your legs sound?"

"Yes, they have received no wound."

"Good. Because I want you to use them. This boy will be your eyes. He will lead you back to Sparta."

"I will not desert my companions," Aristodemos protested.

"Will you honor my orders?" Leonidas demanded.

Aristodemos lowered his head. "Yes, o king."

"Then do as I say. First of all, return the boy to his barracks. See that he is punished for running off." I glanced up quickly, and even in the moonlight I could see that he was serious. "They will flog him. Five strikes for every day missing. See that they flog him for only the day he ran off. He fought as one of us and killed his first Persians. May there be many more to follow. Boy," he said, turning to me, "you will take your strikes like a man. Not a sound."

"Not a sound, o king," I murmured.

"Furthermore, Aristodemos, upon your return to Sparta, tell them what you've seen. Tell them what force Xerxes brings against us. Exhort them to place every man who can bear arms into the field. Will you do this?"

"Yes, my king."

"And tell them that we have remained here at the Hot Gates, obedient to the common law of Sparta. Will you do that?"

"Yes, my king," Aristodemos said, his voice choking over.

"Then be gone," Leonidas said. "The night will be short enough, and they will attack with first light. Your way is long and now even longer with only one sound pair of eyes between you. Be gone, and may Hermes guide and protect you."

Leonidas didn't wait for any response. He had disappeared into the night.

"My shield," Aristodemos said. "If I do not have my shield, they will think I ran away. I will be accused of cowardice. I must have my shield."

"I shall fetch it," I said. "Remain here, and I will return with it." I understood his concern. A man who runs from battle throws away his shield to run more quickly. A Spartan never runs. He returns carrying his shield—or lying dead upon it.

As I made my way back towards the entrance to the passage, I passed by men armed with short swords and shields walking towards the battlefield. I had thought that all the Greeks but the Thespians were leaving. I stopped a man to question him.

"From what city do you hail?" I asked.

"We are from Sparta," the man said. Sparta? Yet these were not hoplites, but lightly armed soldiers. Then I realized who these men were. They were our own helots, our slaves, going to fight beside their masters. The hoplites would not stand alone.

I had only gone a short way through the passage when my father, coming from our camp, found me. He had a shield slung over his shoulder.

"Leonidas sent me with this for Aristodemos," he said. "He told me you are taking him home. You will carry it for him so he may return with honor." He handed me the shield. I stood there, not knowing what to say.

"Be brave," he said, his strong hand on my shoulder. "Be praiseworthy. Speak at home of what we have done here. And now go and do what your king has ordered you." And with no further word, he turned from me and disappeared in the darkness of the Hot Gates.

HISTORICAL NOTES

The battle of Thermopylae (which is Greek for *Hot Gates*) is one of the most stirring stories to come out of ancient history. The story as told here, as well as facts about life in Sparta, are accurate. The Spartan boy Agis, however, is an invention. Although their names are Spartan, his father, as well as his companions, are also inventions. However, it is recorded that a Spartan hoplite named Aristodemos was blinded in one eye during the battle and was subsequently sent back home to report what had happened to his fellow Spartans.

The Persian king Xerxes had inherited an already expanding kingdom from his father Darius. King Darius had invaded Greece in an attempt to add the scattered Greek city-states to his realm. He met defeat at the hands of the Athenians at the Battle of Marathon in 490 BC, an event worth a story of its own and commemorated today every time a marathon race is held.

When Xerxes took over his father's kingdom, he was determined to add the upstart Greeks to his empire. He wanted to follow in his father's footsteps and continue the invasion of mainland Europe. Persia had already absorbed at least forty neighboring nations in Asia Minor, including many Greek colonies in the eastern Mediterranean, the Ionians.

According to ancient historians, Xerxes crossed over into Greece with a combined force of somewhere between two and five million soldiers. Modern historians consider this figure too large and believe that Xerxes' forces numbered at least 60,000 and no more than 300,000. Even the conservative number is an imposing figure for these ancient times.

The Battle of Thermopylae took place on August 11, 480 BC. The facts of the battle, as presented in the story, follow historical accounts. An emissary from Xerxes did offer Leonidas kingship over all of Greece, and he responded as the story tells. When told to give up his arms, King Leonidas reportedly did say, "Come and take them." This phrase is used today on the emblem for the Greek First Army Corps. When the Spartans were threatened that the Persian arrows would blot out the sun, a hoplite from the ranks reportedly commented, "So much the better; we shall fight in the shade." This phrase is nowadays the motto of the Greek 20th Armored Division.

In this story, King Leonidas instructed Aristodemos to return home and tell their people that they had remained at the Hot Gates, "obedient to the common law of Sparta." I took this from an epitaph written by the ancient Greek poet Simonides. This epitaph is engraved in marble and lies today at the site of the ancient battle.

Translated, it reads,

"Go tell the Spartans, O stranger passing by,
That here, obedient to their laws, we lie."

The Spartan sacrifice at Thermopylae was not given in vain. It gave the Athenians enough time to prepare for the Persian invasion. The Persian land force, however, proved to be irresistable. Athens was sacked. The Athenians put their faith in their ships and managed to defeat the immense Persian navy at the Battle of Salamis, off the coast of Athens, under the brilliant leadership of the Athenian general Themistocles. He was a colorful and controversial character, following a shadowy path of intrigue and suspected betrayal, yet led the Greeks to victory. Xerxes fled after this defeat, but left his army behind to ravage and destroy the countryside. Those forces were then defeated and dispersed the following year at the Battle of Plataea by a Greek army collected from numerous city-states. It was, sadly, one of the last times the ancient Greek city-states fought as a unified force.

The Spartans were unique among the Greeks for their practice of enlisting every male citizen as a life-long soldier. Sparta was proud that it had no defensive walls around it. They boasted that the Spartan soldiers were their walls. The cost of this system was that in order to provide food and basic necessities, the Spartans held a whole population of slaves, the helots, that actually outnumbered the citizens.

In contrast to the Spartan practice, other city-states, such as Athens, trained their young men in the arts of war and then released them to follow a profession or continue their family livelihood as farmers and herders. They kept their arms at home and were available in times of emergency as a citizen army.

Following the eventual defeat of Xerxes' army, Athens and Sparta arose as the two dominant powers of Greece. They vied for allies to strengthen and defend their own way of life, and doomed Greece to a generation of destructive civil war, Greek against Greek. Xerxes' invasion had served to strengthen the Greeks. However, they did not know how to deal with the power vacuum after the Persians were expelled, and their incessant in-fighting left them weakened from within.

If you are interested in a rich imagination of how it might have been to live at this time, I recommend Mary Renault's book *The Last of the Wine*. It gives a picture of life at that time from an Athenian perspective and how they viewed the Spartans during the great Peloponnesian Wars.

⇢⇥ ⇤⇠

NOTES ON THE TEXT

p. 6 *Thanatos*.

Translated, this word means "death." The Greeks personified natural forces and addressed them as individual spiritual beings. The boy at this moment is invoking Death, fearing that he is about to be run through with a sword.

p. 8 "I'm guessing an escaped slave."

Slavery was a common practice in ancient Greece. In Athens at its height, it has been estimated that every free family owned at least one slave. Slaves pervaded every aspect of society. They worked as domestics, as workmen for craftsmen and in shops, on farms, and in large groups in mines. Slaves were not commonly foreigners, but rather fellow Greeks. Having a Greek slave gave the benefit that there was no language barrier to overcome. Slaves were acquired as plunder in war (in other words, taken captive and sold or kept as a slave), through piracy on sea as well as kidnapping on land and through both domestic international trade. Their treatment ran the gamut from being part of the family to brutal abuse and oppression. Their status ranged from being kept in chains for forced hard labor (as in the silver mines) to free movement in society with the ability to marry and have a family. For all the autonomy a slave might be permitted, the one area of activity forbidden to a slave was politics.

p. 8 "A helot slave or a Spartan?"

The Spartans had a unique approach to slavery. Personal property was kept to a minimum in their highly communal society. However, since every free Spartan male was trained to be a life-long warrior, they needed a solution for the work that in other cities was normally performed by the men. The answer was to enslave the surrounding population of the part of Greece where Sparta is located, called Laconia. This enslaved population is collectively referred to as helots. They were tied to the land working agriculturally as well as domestically and provided the Spartans with their daily needs. They vastly outnumbered the Spartan population, but what chance did they have for exerting their independence against a highly armed and skillfully trained militia? The Spartans lived in constant fear of rebellion, which broke out on occasion. To prevent the call for freedom from sweeping among the population, the Spartans, freely using spies, regularly culled the more vocal helots. By law, a Spartan could kill a helot without provocation, cause or repercussion.

p. 10 "We all stole food in my *agela*."

At the age of seven, a Spartan boy's ties to his family were broken and he was taken to a state-run camp, joining in a collective called the *agela*, overseen by a twenty-year old. Each *agela* was broken down further into packs of six, called *bouai*, with a leader assigned to each of them. The boys grew up in this barracks life and received their training at arms until they were twenty years old and considered adults.

p. 11 "I'm tired of barley cakes. Let's make a black broth out of him."

The standard diet for a soldier on the march was barley cakes. They were easy to prepare. Barley was roasted and then ground, mixed with water and olive oil and then kneaded into patties; they could be made sweet with honey or savory with salt and onions. Meals were not provided on a march, and soldiers had to bring, buy or steal the food needed along the campaign trail. The Spartans, on the other hand, had their helots to provide them with meals. The Spartans were well known for a peculiar dish of their own, the black broth. It was a soup made from water, blood, vinegar and salt, with a small amount of wild boar meat added. Even in ancient times, this soup was considered something you had to have eaten since childhood in order to stomach.

p. 15 "Hoplites in red capes converged on us from all sides."

A hoplite was an armed foot soldier in ancient Greece. The term *hoplite* was a reference to the type of shield they carried, not that they could *hop lightly*. In fact, the opposite was true. A hoplite's standard armor consisted of a helmet, a breastplate, shin guards called *greaves* and a shield. The helmet weighed five pounds, the bronze breastplate armor between 40–50 pounds, and the shield anywhere from 16–33 pounds. His weapons consisted of a spear, that could be as long as nine feet, and a short sword for stabbing or a weapon specifically for hacking.

p. 16 *Eu-ge!*

This is the ancient Greek equivalent of the modern day Marine Corps exclamation "ooh-rah," barked when troops want to voice approval or a sense of *esprit de corps*. The pronunciation is challenging for English speakers. *Eu* is a diphthong, meaning that both vowels are clearly spoken. Phonetically, it would sound like: "Ay-ooo." The second half of the phrase is *ge*. The pronunciation is as in the English word 'get,' if one leaves off the 't.'

p. 20 "They stood shoulder to shoulder in the phalanx."

A phalanx refers to a military formation of heavily armed infantry where the men are massed in a roughly rectangular shape to prevent enemy troops from penetrating into the ranks.

p. 21 "What the priestess of Apollo in Delphi declares is no secret."

The priestess of Apollo in Delphi was commonly called the Pythia. She was the oracle of Apollo and the most prestigious and authoritative oracle in ancient Greece. Her prophecies were considered so accurate that she was visited not only by Greeks, but by foreign dignitaries who knew they could rely on the information she provided. Her oracles were often spoken in riddle form, offering a double meaning. The prophecy referred to in this story was one of her less ambiguous utterings.

p. 23 "Citizens of Thespiae, no doubt."

The ancient Greek world was not unified under one ruler until the conquests of Philip of Macedon, followed by his son, Alexander the Great. Before that time, Greeks lived in independent city-states, each one called a *polis*. Each polis was self-governing, had its own economy, coinage, culture, religious life and citizen army. Some were democratically organized, such as Athens; others were run by a single ruler, called a tyrant, sometimes benevolent, sometimes not. Many forms existed in between, often involving a council of elders or wealthy citizens.

p. 25 "Our Ephors were hesitant to send any force at all."

    The Ephors were a council of five men who ruled Sparta together with the kings. Sparta had the unique distinction of keeping two kings on the throne, as the story tells us, one to send into the field on campaigns, the other to hold the integrity and safety of the city.

p. 25 "We need the Athenians to stop them before they reach the Isthmus, as they did once before at Marathon."

    The Isthmus is a broad land bridge connecting mainland Greece with the southern peninsula, known as the Peloponnese. Sparta is located in the southern region of the Peloponnese.

    The mention of Marathon is in reference to the earlier Persian invasion of Greece, ten years before. At the epic battle at Marathon, the greatly outnumbered Athenians repelled the Persian fleet from making a landfall, driving them back into the sea.

p. 30 "It's as if we would send the *perioikoi* to battle."

    The *perioikoi* were the people living on the fringe of Sparta. They were neither helots, nor were they Spartan citizens, although they were a free people. Their towns offered a buffer between Sparta proper and the outside world and kept a loose ring around the helot territory, discouraging them from abandoning their duties. Among them were craftsmen and merchants who lived a normal Greek life and provided the Spartans with items they did not make or trade for with the outside world.

p. 33 "I spoke a brief prayer to the nymph of the pools and quickly dipped my fingertips into the hot water to seal my words."

For the Greeks, all of nature was alive with in-dwelling spirits (see note above for *Thanatos*, page 6). In the case of a tree or a body of water, the individualized in-dwelling spirit was, respectively, a dyad or a nymph.

p. 39 "Leonidas went out to meet them. He, too, had been exercising, and he stood there naked…"

It was common among Greek men to exercise and compete in games without any clothing. As we see in the statues that have survived, they considered the well-proportioned male human form an object of beauty and not an expression of sexuality.

p. 39 "They were clearly barbarians."

We use the term *barbarian* in English to refer to a person or culture which we perceive as uncivilized. Not so for the Greeks. A barbarian was simply someone who did not speak Greek and whose language sounded to their ears like "bar-bar-bar," hence the word *barbar*-ian. In fact, the Greeks had a saying: Whoever is not a Greek is a barbarian.

p. 51 "If they find a way to come in behind us, it will be our last battle."

Many Greeks fell to the temptation of siding with the Persians, who they were convinced would be victorious. In this case, a certain Ephialtes, hoping to be richly rewarded, betrayed the location of a goat path that led over the mountains and would bring the Persian troops behind the defending Spartan force. Treason, however, has its own rewards. When the Persians were later defeated at the battle of Salamis, and Xerxes gave up his ambition to add the difficult Greeks to his empire, Ephialtes was never paid. In fact, his identity became known, and the Spartans put a price on his head. He fled and was later murdered for unrelated reasons. The Spartans, we are told, paid the bounty nonetheless, content that the Erinyes, the avenging goddesses of blood revenge, had been appeased.

ABOUT THE AUTHOR

Raised in Los Angeles, Donald Samson spent the first twelve years of his adult life respectively in a Greek fishing village, a small German border town and finally in the mountains of Switzerland.

Mr. Samson has taught in Waldorf schools since 1989. He was a Waldorf class teacher for nineteen years, and his teaching experience spans grades 1–12. His interest in things Greek goes back to his college days when he took up the daunting task of learning ancient Greek.

Mr. Samson has written plays for grades 3–7 and two plays for adults, one of which was a finalist in the Moondance Film Festival. His published works include two translations of Jakob Streit's biblical stories, *Journey to the Promised Land* and *We Will Build a Temple*, and he was a contributing author to *Gazing into the Eyes of the Future, the Enactment of Saint Nicholas in the Waldorf School*. He is author of the award winning fantasy series *The Star Trilogy: The Dragon Boy, The Dragon of Two Hearts* and *The Dragon, the Blade and the Thread*. All these titles are available from AWSNA Publications.

Mr. Samson lives with his family along the Front Range of the Rocky Mountains. You can visit him at www.thedragonboy.com.

⇒≫‒≪⇐

ABOUT THE ILLUSTRATOR

Adam Agee grew up with his younger sister in a magical grove of oak trees. His mother and father let him keep pet snakes and look for bugs under rocks. They also gave him many art materials, and he lay on the floor for hours, drawing imaginary creatures and machines.

After several years of playing make-believe games amid the dirt, rivers, and trees, Adam and his family moved to Colorado where he attended a Waldorf school. His parents supported him in all sorts of creative ventures, and then he went off to Rhode Island School of Design, and traveled the world.

Adam earns his living by making things beautiful and help-ing friends fulfill their creative dreams. He is inspired by the adventure-some stories Mr. Samson writes. Other AWSNA books Adam has illustrated include Donald Samson's *Star Trilogy* and Jakob Streit's *Geron and Virtus*.

When he is not drawing Spartans, Adam spends his time playing Irish fiddle, riding the unicycle, programming web applications, designing graphics, befriending cats, printing on his letterpress, and making up a new language with his sister. You can get a peek into his work at: www.adamagee.com.

-≫-≪-